AILEEN FISHER

I Stood Upon A Mountain

PICTURES BY BLAIR LENT

Thomas Y. Crowell   New York

Library of Congress Cataloging in Publication Data

Fisher, Aileen Lucia.
I stood upon a mountain.
SUMMARY: Standing on top of a mountain, a young
child wonders about the creation of the world.
1. Creation—Juvenile literature. [1. Creation]
I. Lent, Blair, illus. II. Title.
BL226 F57   213   79-3983
ISBN 0-690-03977-8   ISBN 0-690-03978-6 (lib. bdg.)
First Edition

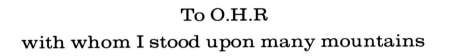

To O.H.R
with whom I stood upon many mountains

I stood upon a mountain
when the year was spring
and dwarf forget-me-nots
scented the air with spice.

A great blue shell of sky
curved above me.
Hills of pine and fir
swelled green below me,
and in the valleys between
I saw mirrors for the sun.

How did it all happen?
I wondered.

An old man came along the trail
and sat on a stone to rest,
his knapsack beside him.
His eyes were full of the blue of sky
and the blue of distance.

"Wonderful world!" I said
by way of greeting.

He nodded. "And to think
it all came from an egg."

"An egg?"

"So I have read,"
the old man told me.
"In the beginning
the world was nothing.
Then slowly
it turned into a great egg.
After a time
the egg split in half.
One of the shells became silver,
and that is the earth.
The other became gold,
and that is the sky.
The fluid between
became the ocean.
And from the yolk
the sun was born."

"Can it be true?" I asked.
For I still wondered.
What had turned nothing
into an egg
in the first place?

I stood upon the seashore
early in the morning
of a summer day.

The gray-green of the sky
and the gray-green of the sea
met in a thin line,
the one like the other.
But the sea was alive.
Its pulse beat upon the shore.

How did it all happen?
I wondered.

A woman came along the beach,
looking for shells.
The tracks of her bare feet
melted behind her.
Eagerly she stooped
to pick up a sand dollar
with a flower on its face.

"Wonderful world!" I said
by way of greeting.

She smiled at me.
"And to think
it all came from a Word."

"A Word?"

"Haven't you heard?" she asked,
looking beyond me to the sea.
" 'In the beginning was the Word,
and the Word was with God,
and the Word was God.'
All things were made by Him,"
she explained.
"That is how it all began."

"It is a good explanation,"
I said.
But still I wondered.
How did the Word begin
in the beginning?

I walked upon the desert
in the brightness
of an autumn afternoon.

The face of the sand
lay wrinkled below me.
It had no place to hide
from the sun.
In the distance
mountains bluer than the sky
curved around the circle
of the world.

How did it all happen?
I wondered.

An Indian walked toward me,
And I went to meet him.
Around his head
he wore a band of red
the color of a cactus flower.
His hair shone black
as a raven's wing.

"Wonderful world!" I said
by way of greeting.

"And to think," he said,
"it all began with fire."

"With fire?"

"In the beginning
came a world of fire,"
he told me.
"That was the first.
From the world of fire,
the world of air broke away.
From the clouds in the air
came the world of water.
Fire, air, water...
and now earth.
The great four."

I nodded.
But still I wondered.
What made the world of fire
in the beginning?

I stood upon a hilltop
at the edge of town
one night in winter
when the moon was half.

Below me
streetlights twinkled like stars.
Above me
the great city of the sky
was ablaze with candles.
An owl talked about it
to a pine tree.

How did it all happen?
I wondered.

I heard voices.
A boy and a girl,
scattering the star-dusted snow
as they climbed,
came to my hilltop.

"Wonderful world!" I said
by way of greeting.

They gazed at a planet
that shone like a bright light
among the smaller star-candles.

"And to think
it all came
from an explosion,"
said the boy.

"An explosion?"

"Don't you know?" he asked.
"Millions of years ago,
more millions
than anyone can say,
everything was part
of an enormous mass.
When it exploded
the stars and planets
and galaxies were born."

"The mysterious universe,"
said the girl softly,
as she turned her face up
to look again at the sky.

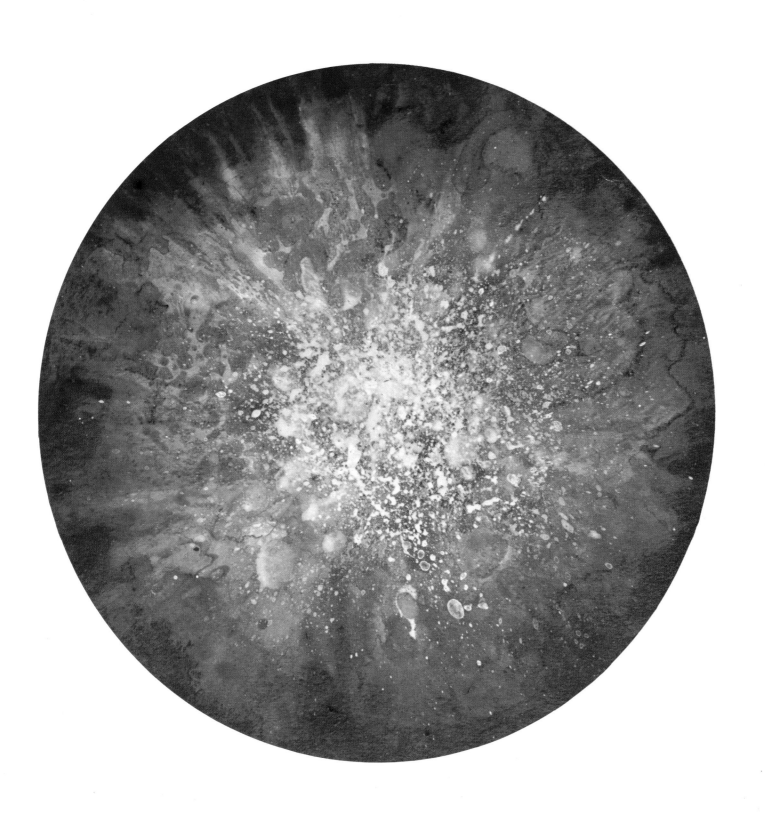

"What an explosion
that must have been!"
I cried.
Yet still I wondered.
Where could such an enormous mass
have come from
in the first place?

An egg
a Word
a world of fire,
an explosion...
there are many answers.

Yet when I stand upon a mountain,
or walk upon the seashore,
or look into the face of the desert,
or climb to a hilltop at night,
I am still
filled with a wonder
that needs no answer,
no answer at all.